KEEPSAKE COLORING BOOK

ILLUSTRATED BY **KATIE COOK**

Los Angeles • New York

 Published by Disney • Lucasfilm Press, an imprint of Disney Book Group. For information address Disney • Lucasfilm Press, 1101 Flower Street, Glendale, California 91201.

Printed in the United States of America

First Edition, September 2017 10 9 8 7 6 5 4 3

Library of Congress Control Number on file

FAC-008598-17332

ISBN 978-1-368-01754-1

Designed by Leigh Zieske

Visit the official *Star Wars* website at: www.starwars.com.

STAR WARS

STAR WARS

STAR WARS

STAR WARS

STAR WARS

STAR WARS

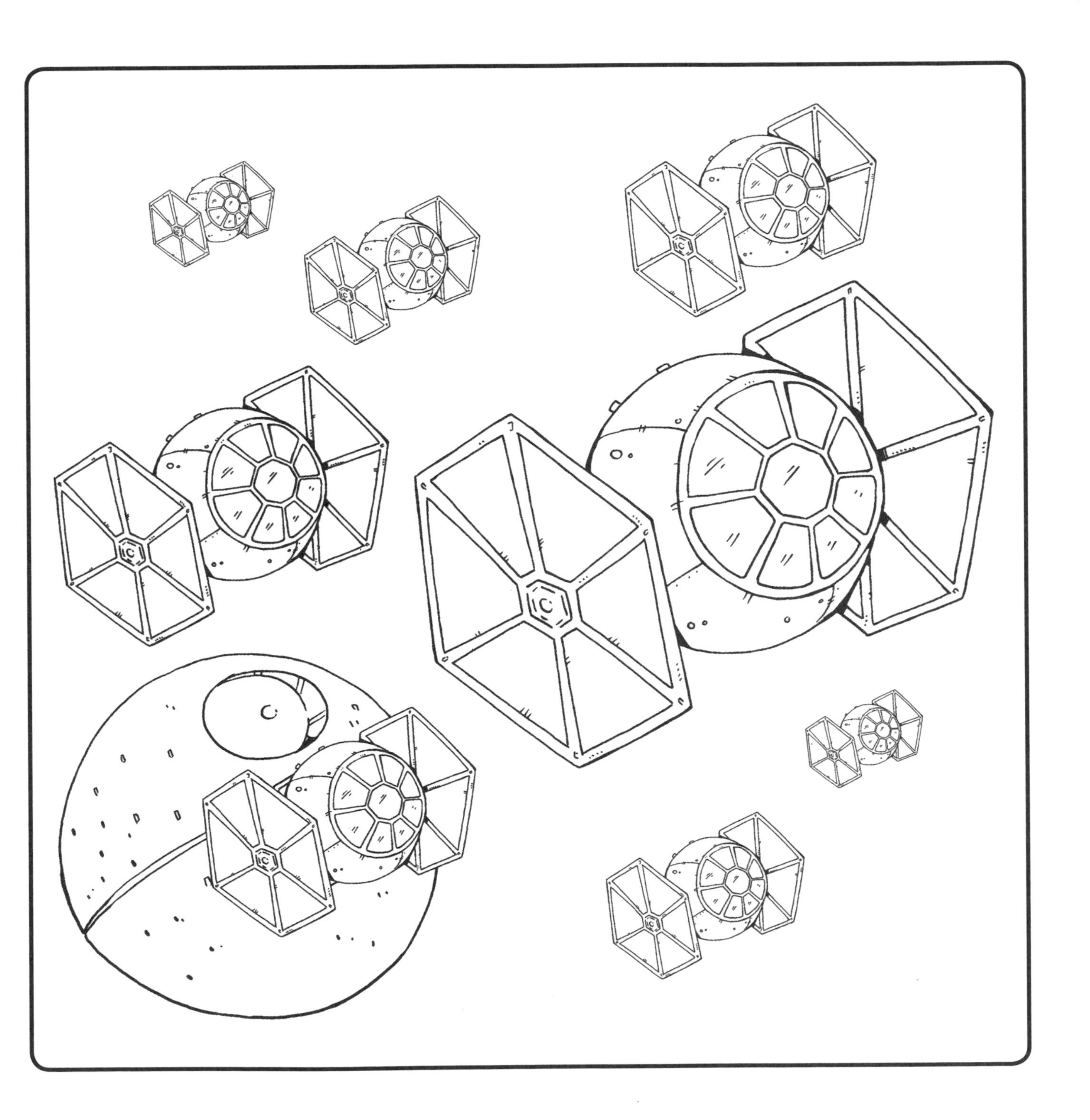

STAR WARS

STAR WARS

NOOO!

STAR WARS

I DON'T WANT TO SAY THE THING!
SAY THE THING!

STAR WARS

STAR WARS

STAR WARS

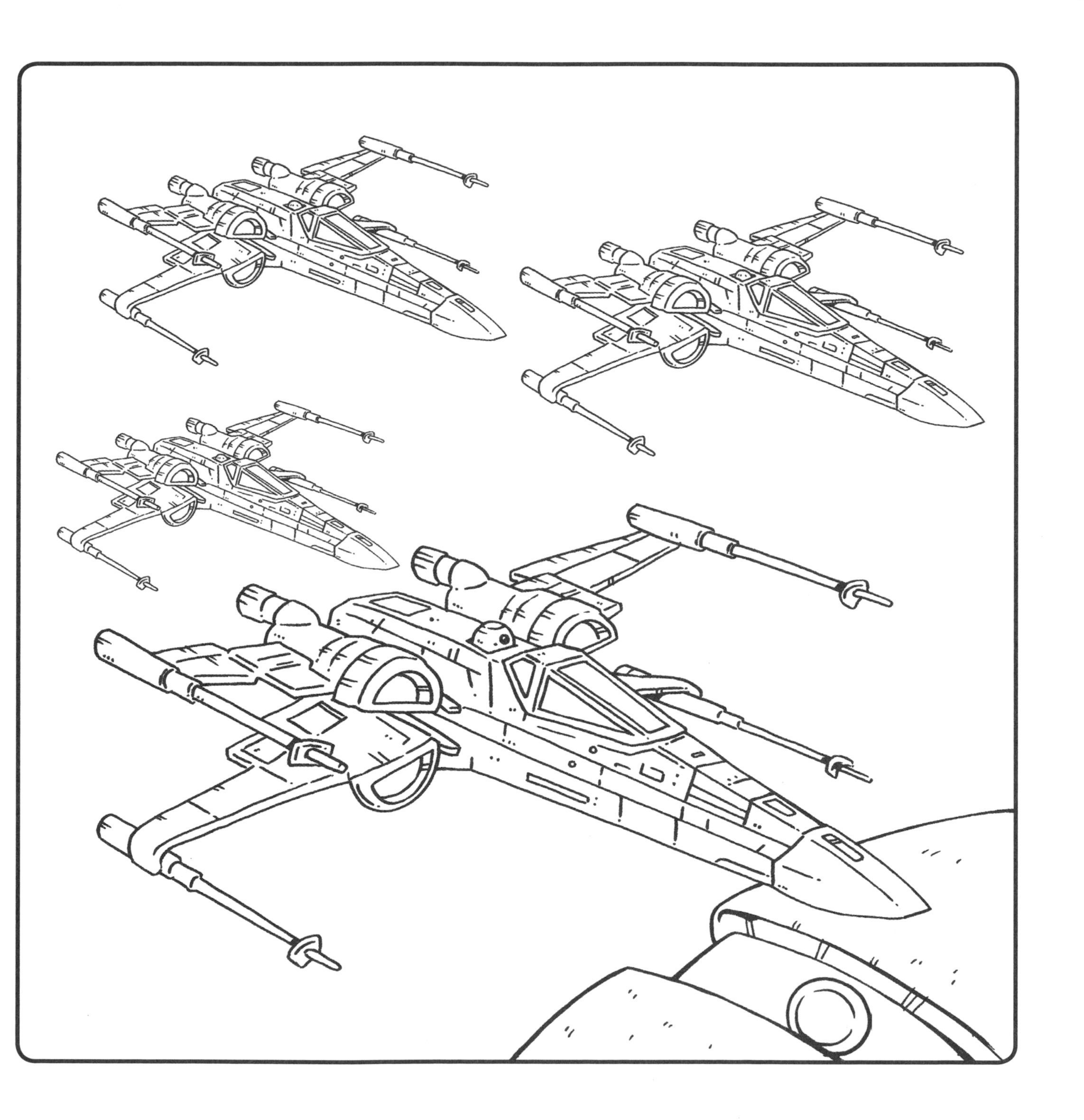

STAR WARS

STAR WARS

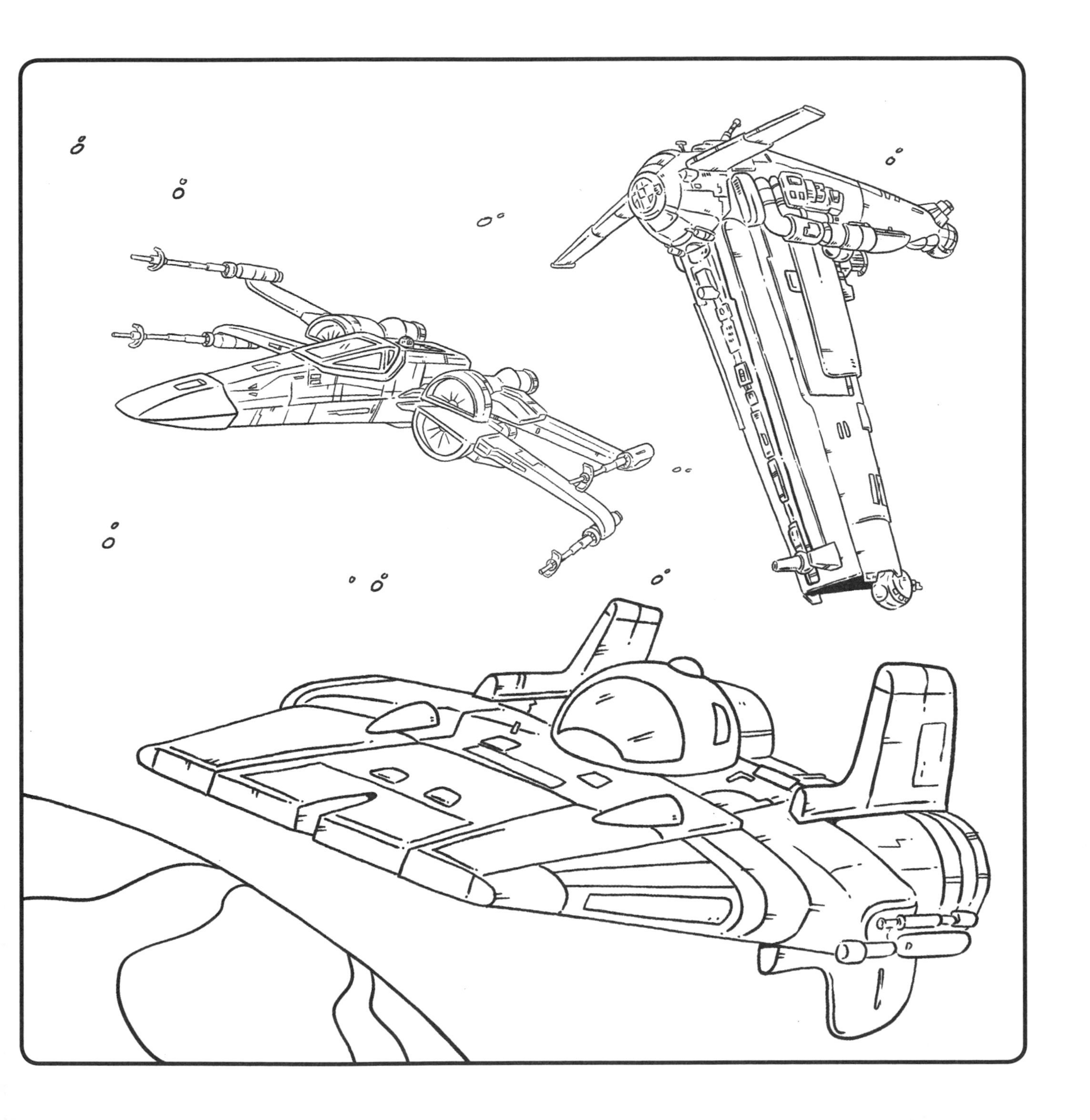

STAR WARS